THE SCARED
SCARECROW

THE SCARED SCARECROW

First printed 2015

Copyright © 2015 by Lynda Gray

Author: Lynda Gray
Illustrator: Oogaboo Art Studio.
Pasadena, California
Designer: Selah Dimech
Project Editor: Danielle Barone

ISBN: 978-1511611329

lyndagrayauthor.com

THE SCARED SCARECROW

Lynda Gray

LYNDA GRAY

Once there was a scared scarecrow.

He did not like scaring the crows.

He did not like scaring the rabbits.

He was frightened.

He tried to be like all
the other scarecrows.

He went to scarecrow school.
He copied what they did!

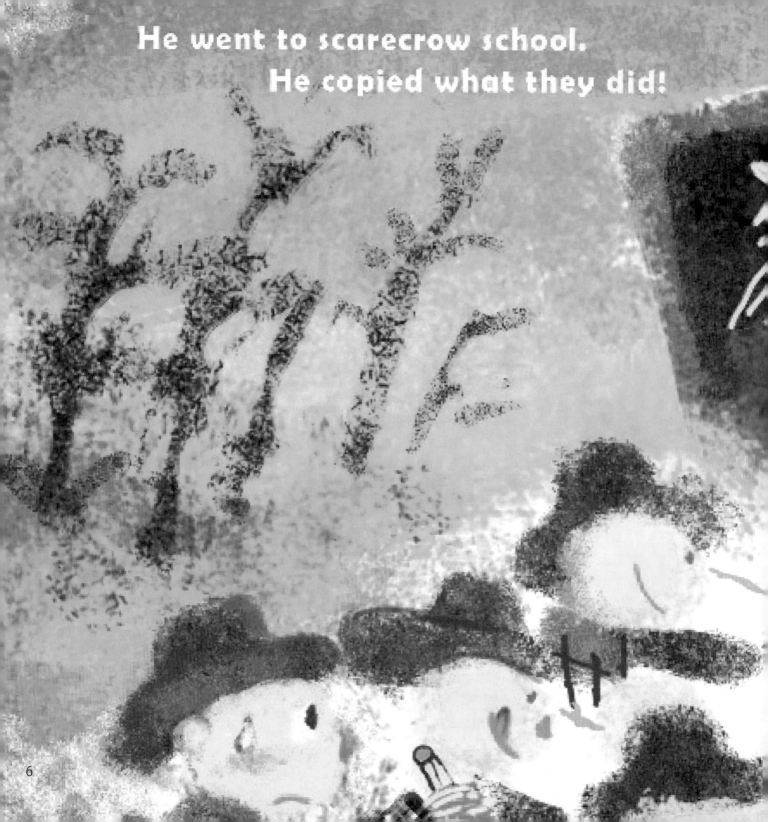

The other scarecrows laughed.

When the crows came to eat all the farmer's crops, he stood still and shivered.

One day there was a thumping noise
from the farmyard. HOP! HOP! HOP!

All the other scarecrows looked up from their perches ready to go to battle.

11

But not the scared scarecrow
he hid in the barn.

The thumping noise grew louder and louder.

Suddenly one hundred rabbits hopped over the hill.

The sheep's baaed, the cows mooed,
the horses neighed, the roosters crowed
COCK A DOODLE DOO,

mooo
moooo

baa
baa

14

neigh

but nothing would stop

those hungry rabbits.

Cock a Doodle Doo

15

Until, out of the barn crept the scared Scarecrow.

He whispered to himself, I can do it, I can do it.

16

SHOO...SHOO

SHOO...SHOO

SHOO...SHOO

You Rabbits - You

SHOO...

SHOO...

17

The rabbits looked up at the scared Scarecrow and fled.

18

Altogether,

the sheeps baaed

the cows mooed,

the horses neighed,

the roosters crowed

COCK A DOODLE DOO,

to thank the scared Scarecrow.

19

He is now a hero, standing tall on his perch.

And he will always be remembered
for saving the farm

during the Battle of the Rabbits.

50504831R00018

Made in the USA
San Bernardino, CA
24 June 2017